THE SUMMER EXPLORERS

Plays by Cath Howe

Illustrated by Roger Simó

Metal Detectives 3
Night Visitor 18

Published by Pearson Education Limited, Edinburgh Gate, Harlow, Essex, CM20 2JE.

www.pearsonschools.co.uk

Text © Pearson Education Limited 2013
Designed by Georgia Styring
Original illustrations © Pearson Education 2013
Illustrated by Roger Simó, Advocate-Art Agency

The right of Cath Howe to be identified as author of this work has been asserted by her in accordance with the Copyright, Designs and Patents Act 1988.

First published 2013

17 16 15 14 13
10 9 8 7 6 5 4 3 2 1

British Library Cataloguing in Publication Data
A catalogue record for this book is available from the British Library

ISBN 978 0 435 14416 6

Printed and bound in the UK by Ashford Colour Press.

Acknowledgements
We would like to thank Bangor Central Integrated Primary School, Northern Ireland; Bishop Henderson Church of England Primary School, Somerset; Bletchingdon Parochial Church of England Primary School, Oxfordshire; Brookside Community Primary School, Somerset; Bude Park Primary School, Hull; Carisbrooke Church of England Primary School, Isle of Wight; Cheddington Combined School, Buckinghamshire; Dair House Independent School, Buckinghamshire; Deal Parochial School, Kent; Glebe Infant School, Goucestershire; Henley Green Primary School, Coventry; Lovelace Primary School, Surrey; Our Lady of Peace Junior School, Slough; Tackley Church of England Primary School, Oxfordshire; and Twyford Church of England School, Buckinghamshire for their invaluable help in the development and trialling of the Bug Club resources.

Every effort has been made to contact copyright holders of material reproduced in this book. Any omissions will be rectified in subsequent printings if notice is given to the publishers.

Metal Detectives

Characters

Sofia
— sister of Pablo

Pablo
— brother of Sofia

Miranda
— sister of Rico

Rico
— brother of Miranda

George
— brother of Eden

Eden
— sister of George

Six children are walking along a beach.
Miranda is holding a metal detector.

Rico: I promised the grown-ups we'd all stay together. We can go as far as those rocks over there.

Pablo: What have you got there, Miranda?

Miranda: It's a metal detector.

Pablo: What does it do?

Eden: Detects metal, you banana.

Miranda: My dad says we can try it out.

George: So how does the ... err ... the defector work?

Miranda: **Detector**! You press this button here, then kind of hover it over the ground, and that red light flashes if it finds metal.

Sofia: I've got a pin in my leg where I broke it. Will it detect that?

Pablo: Let's see. Yeah, look, it's flickering.

5

Rico: This section of beach has lots of fossils, according to my guidebook.

Eden: Not metal ones, though.

Rico: Someone found a dinosaur fossil here, near the cliffs. I've got some bags in case we find fossils, or shells, or plants, or ...

George: Has anyone got any food?

Eden: Here, you can have my jam sandwich.

Pablo: Hey, the light's flashing!

George: Did the metal detector find something? What is it?

Pablo: Just a rusty old bottle top.

Sofia: It's my turn to try now.

Pablo: No it's not. It's still mine!

Sofia: You've had ages!

Pablo: That's not true!

Eden: Stop arguing! What's wrong, Sofia?

Sofia: My feet are killing me.

Miranda: Where are your boots?

Sofia: Here, in my rucksack.

Rico: Well, why don't you put them on? It's rocky; no wonder your feet are sore.

Sofia: Yeah, well, I wish I could wear them, but something's happened to this one. Look.

George: The leather's torn.

Eden: And look at the lace!

Sofia: I left them outside the cottage last night and when I got up, the lace was in three bits. Now they just keep coming undone.

Pablo: Well, I didn't do it.

Sofia: My dad said he thought it might have been a fox. They chew things. Anyway, now my boot's useless.

George: Didn't you bring any other shoes?

Sofia: I can't find my trainers.

Rico: Well, put your boots on anyway, even if they won't both do up.

Miranda: Hey, give me a go with the metal detector. I'm going to take it around that rock pool.

George: What's the best thing you've ever found with the metal detector, Miranda? Any treasure?

Miranda: We once found a screwdriver down behind the shed in our garden.

Pablo: It sounds more like a rubbish detector, then.

George: If there used to be pirates here, we might find their treasure.

Miranda: Oh wow!

(She bends down to pick up something.)

Oh no, it's just a can.

Eden: Maybe it's a pirate can.

Rico: What's this? The metal detector's flashing again.

Miranda: It's ... it's a bowl of some kind with holes and a black handle.

Eden: It's so crusty. The seaweed's all dried round it.

Rico: It's a bashed kettle! It's lost its spout.

Pablo: Did pirates have kettles?

Rico: I don't think so. Still, we could take it back … wash it?

George: It's got loads of holes.

Miranda: Maybe it could be a sprinkler … a kettle watering can sprinkler.

Pablo: This metal detector's useless. Who wants a stupid metal kettle with no spout?

Eden: Well, **I** like it.

Pablo: Just a sec – what's that sticking up over there?

Rico: It's a seagull.

Pablo: No, behind the seagull.

George: A shark fin.

Miranda: Sharks don't bury themselves in sand.

George: Maybe it's asleep.

Pablo: Come on; it's something big. The metal detector's flashing like mad – look.

Eden: You're right.

Sofia: Let's dig it out!

They all start digging.

Miranda: It's too far down.

Pablo: It's coming up!

Eden tugs at something and falls back, clutching their find to her chest.

Eden: It's ... I think it's a lantern.

Miranda: Eugh! It's full of smelly shells and weed.

Rico: I love the carved bits, though. And look, here. There's some kind of writing.

George: Oh yeah. Let's clean it out when we get back.

14

Miranda: Look, there's a little window you can open. Maybe you could put a candle inside.

Eden: You're right; there's even some old melted wax.

Sofia: It looks ... creepy, somehow. All that dark writing.

Pablo: I wonder whose it was.

George: We could try putting a candle inside it tonight.

Sofia: Hey, I've found something else! It's got loads of weed stuck to it.

Miranda: It's a brooch!

Pablo examines the brooch, unimpressed.

He answers sarcastically.

Pablo: So it is! This is better than Christmas ...

Sofia: Don't be like that, Pablo. This is really good! If I clip it to my boot ... here, and then wind this long bit of seaweed through the lace holes ...

George: You've invented a new kind of shoelace!

Sofia: The buckle thing's cool, though. I think it's from a pirate.

Miranda: We present: Sofia's sensational pirate-and-seaweed boots. Give us a twirl!

Sofia twirls and stumbles on the rocks.

Rico: The grown-ups are waving for us to go back. Let's show them.

George: I'll carry the lantern.

16

Sofia starts to run.

Sofia: Race you all back.

Eden: Wait for us!

Night Visitor

Characters

Pablo
– brother of Sofia

Sofia
– sister of Pablo

Miranda
– sister of Rico

Rico
– brother of Miranda

George
– brother of Eden

Eden
– sister of George

Six children are sitting in a holiday cottage, playing a game of cards. It is starting to get dark.

Pablo: I keep dropping my cards.

Rico: I've been keeping mine in that kettle we found on the beach.

Sofia glares at Pablo.

Sofia: Cheat!

Pablo: No, I'm not!

Sofia: You **are**! You found that card on the floor.

Pablo: I dropped it, that's all.

Sofia: Yeah, right!

Rico: Stop fighting, you two!

George: I'm starving! When's the food ready?

Rico: My dad's making baked potatoes.

Miranda: I hope we can roast marshmallows again tonight.

Eden: Did you clean the lantern we found, George?

George: Yeah. My mum put a candle in it. It's on the windowsill, look.

Eden: Right, I've got Mr and Mrs Monkey and two baby monkeys.
(She makes a monkey noise.)
Safari family! I've got no cards left. I win!

Sofia: You always win, Eden.

Pablo: It's just luck.

Sofia: It's getting really dark outside.

George: Look, the lantern's flickering. It makes the old writing around the edge light up.

Eden: People used to signal with lanterns. Ships used to follow the lights to the harbour, especially if it was foggy.

Miranda: It's foggy tonight, isn't it?

Eden: I suppose so.

Pablo: It feels ... cold.

Sofia: I like watching that lantern but, well, it makes me wonder ... could the lantern's owner come back for it?

Miranda: What do you mean?

Sofia: Well, something outside might be watching the light.

George: You mean like something ... floating silently towards the house ...

Sofia: That's just rubbish.

George: ... coming back to collect what belongs to him.

Eden: That's creepy. Stop it, you two! Switch the room light on, Pablo.

Pablo tries flicking the switch on the wall.

Pablo: It's not working. The light must need a new bulb.

Rico: Where's your torch, Miranda?

Miranda: Here, in my pocket.

Rico: What was that?

Miranda: What?

George: At the window. I saw it, too! Something flew in.

All: ARGH!

Miranda: It didn't. You're making it up!

Rico: Shine the torch, Miranda.
(He gasps.)
Hanging up in the corner of the window. Look!

Eden:	What is it, Rico?
Rico:	It's a bat!
Pablo:	How did **that** get in?
Rico:	Shush. The window was open, of course.
Eden:	I'll tell Dad.

Eden exits.

Sofia: It's moving!

George: Argh!

Pablo: Everyone duck!

Miranda whispers.

Miranda: Shh, you two; you'll scare it. You've made me drop the torch.

Rico picks up the torch. Eden enters.

Eden: Dad says it's just like when I got a bird in my bedroom. He'll help if we want. Where's the bat gone now?

Sofia: It was over in the corner. Maybe it flapped off home again.

Miranda: I bet it's still in here.

Rico: Bats look for the darkest place in the room and sleep there.

George: There are loads of dark places!

Eden: Shush! Right, let's all spread around the room and gently move things. How about down behind this cupboard?

Rico: Be careful, Eden!

Sofia: What if it bites you?

Eden: Don't worry, Sofia.

George: That's it; I'm staying by the door!

Rico: For goodness sake, be quiet!

Miranda: Would it go under the settee? It must be really dark under there.

Pablo: Good idea. Let's move it back.

Sofia: Anything?

Eden: Just an apple core.

Pablo: Yuck!

27

Eden: There's so much rubbish on the floor! Whose cereal bowl is this?

George: Er, mine, I think.

Sofia: What was that noise?

Miranda: Something's plopped onto the floor! Shine the torch!

Pablo: There it is!

They all gasp.

Sofia: Wow! A real bat!

Rico: It's beautiful. So black!

Eden: It's like a mouse, isn't it?

Miranda: And its wings … they're like silk.

George: Maybe it's hurt … or resting.

Pablo: Not for long!

Eden: Look at its eyes shining!

Sofia: Put something on top of it, quick!

Miranda: Will this lunchbox do?

Miranda drops a lunchbox over the bat.

Rico: What's happening?

George: It's dancing inside.

Rico: Push this bit of card under it.

Eden: Three … two … one!

The bat flies away.

Eden: It's gone.

Pablo: That was awesome!

Sofia: Hey, do you really think it was the spirit of the lantern?

Miranda: Don't be daft. It probably just saw the light.

George: It was so ... strange, though, with its folded wings.

Rico: Its eyes were golden.

George: I know it sounds stupid but, well, I'm glad it came.

Pablo: And **I'm** glad it's gone!

Eden: I thought we'd be terrified but in the end it was ... special, wasn't it?

Rico: Beautiful.

Miranda: Like a visitor from ... another world.

George: Another world ... yes.

Pause.

Sofia: Well, will someone please shut the window before its mum arrives?

They all laugh.